MY SON, THE TIME TRAVELLER

"What's your name?" the boy asked.

"Zack," I said.

"Zack? Your name is Zack?" The kid got this strange look on his face. Like he'd seen a ghost or something. "Now I know why you look so familiar! Oh! no! Please, don't be mad at me. Please!"

Mad at him? Why should I be mad at him?

"What's *your* name?" I asked.

"Mack."

I had an eerie feeling.

"Please, don't tell me you're from the parallel universe," I said. "Because I've already been through all that once."

"Don't worry," he said. "I'm not from the parallel universe."

"Well, that's a relief," I said.

"I'm from the future," he said. "I'm your son . . ."

THE ZACK FILES

THE ZACK FILES

MY SON, THE TIME TRAVELLER

DAN GREENBURG

Illustrated by
JACK E. DAVIS

MACMILLAN CHILDREN'S BOOKS

For Judith, and for the real Zack,
with love – DG

Copyright © Dan Greenburg 1997. All rights reserved.
First published in the United States by Grosset & Dunlap.
British publication rights arranged with Sheldon Fogelman.

This edition published 1998 by Macmillan Children's Books
a division of Macmillan Publishers Limited
25 Eccleston Place, London SW1W 9NF
and Basingstoke
Associated companies throughout the world.

ISBN 0 330 35359 4

Illustrations © Jack E Davis 1997

The right of Dan Greenburg to be identified as the
author of this work has been asserted by him in accordance
with the Copyright, Designs and Patents Act 1988

1 3 5 7 9 8 6 4 2

A CIP catalogue record for this book is available fron the British Library

Typeset in Baskerville MT
Printed and bound in Great Britain by Mackays of Chatham plc, Kent

Chapter One

● ● ● ● ●

My name is Zack. And weird stuff follows me around like a puppy. I'm not kidding. For example, the day I'm going to tell you about started out like a pretty normal day. School had just let out. Oh, I forgot to mention. I'm in fifth grade at the Horace Hyde-White School for Boys. That's in New York City, in case you were wondering.

Anyhow, I was on my way to Bats and Stats. It's a really cool store that sells all kinds of baseball stuff. There was this card I'd been saving up for. A Wade Boggs rookie card. It cost thirty dollars. That's way more expensive than any card I own. But my Grandma Leah was in from Chicago for a big family reunion. And she gave me five dollars. So that put me right over the top. Now I had thirty-two dollars and forty-seven cents in my pocket. The Wade Boggs card was going to be mine!

As I went into Bats and Stats, an older kid was leaving. I was in such a hurry, I bumped into him.

"Sorry," I said as I ran inside.

I plunked my money down on the counter.

"OK, Fred," I said to the owner. His name is Fred. "Let's have that Wade Boggs rookie card."

"Too late," said Fred.

"What do you mean?"

"I sold it. To the kid who just left."

"You sold it?" I said. "How could you do that?"

"Sorry, Zack," he said. "I didn't think you'd ever have the money. And I gotta make a living, you know?"

What! I couldn't believe my rotten luck!

I ran out of the store. I wasn't going to let that Wade Boggs rookie card get away. The older kid who'd bought it wasn't even halfway down the block when I caught up with him.

"Excuse me," I said, "but I need to talk to you."

The kid turned around.

"What? Who, me?" He was about thirteen and he looked like a real Yankees fan. He was wearing a team sweatshirt. It said "World Champs 2030". Weird. I thought I'd seen all the Yankee sweatshirts. But I'd never seen that one.

"That Wade Boggs rookie card you just bought," I said. "I'd like to buy it from you."

He shook his head.

"Sorry," he said. He kept on walking. He seemed nervous and in a hurry.

"Listen, I'll pay you more than you bought it for," I said. "I'll give you thirty-one dollars for it."

"Sorry."

He was walking faster now. I had to jog to keep up with him.

"Thirty-two bucks," I said.

He shook his head again. "Hey, I've got to go," he said. "I'm supposed to be back on my tour bus."

"OK," I said. "Thirty-two dollars and forty-seven cents. And that's my final offer. I mean, that's all I have. Honest."

"Listen," he said, "I wouldn't sell this card for thirty-two *hundred* dollars. Which is probably what it's worth."

Thirty-two hundred dollars? Was he crazy or something? Saying the card was worth a hundred times what he paid? He was jogging now. I practically had to run to keep up with him.

"Please! Wade Boggs is my all-time favourite player," I said. "My dream is to play for the Yankees, same as Wade. I really need that card!"

"I need it, too," he said. "I lost one just like it that belonged to my dad. I took it to school to show my friends. It disappeared. I have to get my dad another one before he hears it's gone, or he'll snarz out."

Snarz out? What kind of expression was that? But I could understand this kid's problem. It was like something I'd do myself. Still, I had to have that card.

We got to the end of the block. Cars and trucks whizzed past us. He looked around and frowned.

"It's gone!" he said.

"What? The card?"

"No, the tour bus." He looked pretty upset. "Oh, splendid! I've really done it now! How will I get back?"

"To where?" I was wondering what kind of place this guy was from, where kids said "splendid" and "snarz out".

"You wouldn't understand," he answered.

"Look," I said, "isn't there any way you could sell me that card? Any way at all?"

"I can't," he said. "Wade Boggs is my dad's favourite player of all time. My dad used to go to Yankee games when he was a kid. With *his* dad. I mean, they actually saw Wade Boggs *play*."

"What's the big deal about seeing Wade Boggs play?" I said. "I see Wade Boggs play all the time."

The kid looked even more nervous now. Like he'd said something wrong or something.

"Uh . . . of course you do," he said. "I forgot."

He took a good look at me.

"You know," he said, "you sure do look familiar."

I took a good look at him.

"So do you," I said.

He *did* look like somebody I knew. But I'd never seen him before. He had spiky brown hair, brown eyes, and a thin, pointy nose. All of a sudden I knew who he looked like. Me. An older me. A thirteen-year-old me.

"What's your name?" he asked.

"Zack," I said.

"Zack? Your name is Zack?" The kid got this strange look on his face. Like he'd seen a ghost or something. "Oh, no!" The kid was shaking his head now and backing away from me. "Now I know why you look so familiar! Oh, no! Please, don't be mad at me. Please!"

Mad at him? Why should I be mad at him?

"What's *your* name?" I asked.

"Mack."

"Mack," I repeated.

Then I had an eerie feeling. One morning a couple of months ago, I opened my medicine cabinet door, and there was a kid who looked like me on the other side. His name was Zeke, and he lived in a parallel universe. My dental brace fell into his universe, and it was a whole big deal to get it back.

"Please, don't tell me you're from the parallel universe," I said. "Because I've already been through all that once."

"Don't worry," he said. "I'm not from the parallel universe."

"Well, that's a relief," I said.

"I'm from the future," he said. "I'm your son."

Chapter Two

● ● ● ● ●

"My son?" I said. I stopped dead in my tracks. "Yeah, right. Well, for your information, I'm not even married."

"Of course you're not married," he said. "How could you be married? You're . . ." He looked at a paper at the newsstand on the corner. "OK, this is 1998. So you're . . . what? You're only ten years old, right?"

"And a half," I said.

"OK, ten and a half," he said. "I was born about twenty years from now. I mean, I just left you in the future, and you're like forty-three there."

"You just left me?" I said. "How could I be in two places at once?"

He shook his head.

"Oh, right," he said. "I forgot. You guys didn't understand a thing about time travel back then."

"Back when?" I said.

"Back now. Look, Dad, let me prove it to you. Your father's name is Dan, and he's a writer. Your grandma's name is Leah. Your mom and dad are divorced. Your great-grandpa's name is Maurice, and he was reincarnated as a cat."

I looked at him closely. This kid had really done his homework.

"Knowing all that is impressive," I said. "I admit that. Especially the stuff about my great-grandfather. But it doesn't really prove anything. And it sure doesn't make you my future son."

He sighed.

"Boy, Dad," he said, "I see you were stubborn even as a kid. OK, how's this? I know all about the trip you and your dad took to Hawaii."

Hawaii. That got me. I have never been to Hawaii. Not yet. But just last night my dad told me we'd probably be going there over spring break. He's going to write a story about some volcano or something. How could this kid have found out about that trip?

"Who told you about Hawaii?" I asked.

"You did, Dad. You've been telling me

stories about that trip since I was a little kid!"

Mack reached into his pocket. He took out a wallet and opened it. Inside was this really old photograph. It was cracked and faded. But you could make out two people standing on a beach, with palm trees behind them. One was a dark-haired man in a loud Hawaiian print shirt. The other was a kid wearing lots of flowered necklaces – leis – around his neck. It was me and my dad!

I suddenly found it hard to stand up. Sometimes meeting your future son will do that to you.

"Hey, Dad, are you all right?" he asked worriedly.

"Yeah, yeah," I said. "Whew. This is just a little weird, even for me. You know?"

"I bet. Just take it easy, Dad."

Mack was talking in this very concerned voice. Just the way I do when I see my dad is really upset.

"And it doesn't make it easier that you're older and taller than me either," I said.

Mack nodded.

"I can see that."

"By the way," I said. "What are you doing here?"

"Well, I'm on a class trip. We're here to see what Old New York was like at the turn of the century. Then I saw that baseball store. Here was my big chance. I'd buy another Wade Boggs rookie card – at cheap 1998 prices – to replace the one I lost."

"*Old* New York?"

"Yeah. We teleported here on this

splendid double-decker tour bus. It's a 1998 model – a real antique. It's powered by Vaseline, or gasoline, or something."

"And they actually let you get off this bus to look around on your own?"

Mack looked embarrassed.

"Actually, we're sort of not supposed to get off the bus. They're always warning us terrible things will happen if we do. You know – like we'll de-atomize or something. I think they're just trying to scare us, but —"

"But now the bus is gone."

"Yep."

I could see that my son had a problem.

"Well, do you remember where the bus was going?" I asked. "You could catch up with it at the next stop."

He looked even more embarrassed.

"My teacher gave us all a schedule," he said. "But I think I may have left it on the bus."

I nodded. That's another thing I would have done. This kid really was a lot like me.

"I remember the last stop has something to do with . . . with a clock, I think," he said. Then he shrugged. "I guess that doesn't help much, though."

"Was it by the clock at F.A.O. Schwarz?" I said. That's my favourite toy store.

"I don't think so."

"There's a clock near Macy's that is counting down to the year 2000. Is that it?"

"No, that doesn't sound like it, either," Mack said.

"Well, what happens if you don't meet up with them?"

"Uh . . . I don't think that'd be too good."

"What do you mean?" I said. "Do you mean you'll be trapped in the present?"

"I don't know. I guess so, yeah." He laughed. "Or maybe I'll de-atomize."

I frowned. Mack thought it was funny, but if he missed the bus, wouldn't my grown-up self worry? I know my ten-year-old self was getting plenty worried!

What was I going to do?

Chapter
Three

● ● ● ● ●

Speaking of worrying, I suddenly remembered about Grandma Leah. She's the world champion of worriers.

"Mack, I'm supposed to meet my Grandma Leah at the beauty parlour! I told her I'd be there by four o'clock. After I bought the baseball card."

"Grandma Leah?" His eyes got wide. "*The* Grandma Leah? Splendid!

I'd sure like to meet her!"

I wasn't so sure how Grandma Leah would take to meeting her future great-grandson. But maybe she could help us figure out how to find the tour bus.

"The beauty parlour's just a few blocks away," I said. So we started down the street. Right away I saw Mack didn't have a clue about traffic. Maybe traffic worked differently in the future. I made sure he held my hand crossing all the streets.

"Wow!" he said. "Look at that, Dad!"

He was pointing at the corner. I didn't see anything. Just an old guy walking his dog.

"That guy is bald!" Mack shrieked.

The bald guy gave us this really dirty look.

I hurried Mack down the street.

"So what?" I said.

"So nobody gets bald any more. Dr Harry Ferdfleisch discovered the cure around 2009. His birthplace was the first stop on our tour." Mack took one more look back at the bald guy. "It's so weird to see how people looked in olden times. The past is splendid. Actually, I wouldn't mind staying a while."

I didn't say anything. But in my gut I knew that wasn't such a hot idea. Mack needed to get back where he belonged. In the future.

In a few minutes we arrived at Pierre's Hair Today beauty parlour. Inside, old ladies sat under big, bubble-type hair-dryers, reading magazines. One lady was leaning back over a sink, getting a blue rinse in her hair. There was a framed picture of somebody named Ethel Merman hanging next to the cash register. She had written "Dear Pierre: Luv ya, baby!" across the bottom of it.

We found Grandma Leah sitting in a chrome chair, the kind that goes up and down. A hairdresser guy was fussing over her. She seemed to like being fussed over.

"Zack, dear, hello," she said. "Did you get the baseball card?"

Before I could answer, Grandma Leah turned to the hairdresser guy.

"Mr Pierre, this is my grandson Zack, and . . ." She stopped talking and looked at Mack. "Who is your friend, Zack?"

"Grandma," I said, "this is Mack."

"How do you do, Mack?" she said.

Mack was looking at Grandma Leah like she was a movie star or something.

"Are you the famous Grandma Leah?" he asked.

"Famous?" she said. She looked delighted.

"I've heard so much about you," said Mack. "You're like a legend in my family."

"A legend?" said Grandma Leah.

Mr Pierre finished rolling Grandma Leah's hair in big fat curlers. Then he walked away. Grandma Leah swivelled her chair around.

"This is a lovely young man, Zack," she said. "Is he a friend from school?"

"Uh, not exactly," I said.

"Then where do you know him from, dear?"

I looked at Mack. He shrugged.

Grandma Leah is eighty-eight, but she's a very peppy, open-minded person. I was sure she'd be able to handle hearing who Mack was.

"Grandma," I said, "actually, Mack is my son."

Grandma Leah stared at Mack for a moment in silence. Then she shook her head.

"Zack, don't talk nonsense," she said. "You can't have a son. You're a ten-year-old boy."

"He isn't my son *now*," I said. "He'll be my son when I grow up and get married."

"You mean that then you'll adopt him?" she said. "Somebody older than you are?" She made a sour face. "No, I'm sorry, this just does not seem proper."

"No, no, Grandma Leah," I said. "You don't understand. Mack is my son from the future. He isn't even born yet. He won't be born for another twenty years."

Grandma Leah squinted her eyes and looked at me sharply.

"Tell me," she said, "is this like that business with Great-Grandpa Maurice?"

Did I mention that my Great-Grandpa Maurice was reincarnated as a cat? I think so. Well, anyway, when we brought him to Chicago, Grandma Leah did have a tiny bit of trouble with the whole idea.

"It might be a *little* like the Great-Grandpa Maurice business," I said.

"Then I don't want to hear about it," she said, turning away. "I didn't like that, and I don't like this."

Mr Pierre came back with a huge dryer on a stand. He fitted it over Grandma Leah's head. Then he turned it on. We waited till Mr Pierre left before we went on talking.

"Great-Grandma Leah," said Mack, "I really am Zack's future son. And I'm really glad to meet you."

"Tell him I don't talk to people from the future," said Grandma Leah. She was speaking louder now because of the noise from the hairdryer. "Tell him I don't talk to people from the past, either. It's a rule I have. Tell him I don't even talk to most people from the present."

"Grandma," I said, "Mack needs help."

"If he thinks he's from the future, he needs help, all right," she said. "And you do, too."

"Grandma, he really does need help."

"So let Buck Rogers help him," she said loudly.

"Grandma, listen to me." I didn't want to shout. So I leaned over till I was almost nose-to-nose with her. "Mack got off a tour bus from the future by mistake. And it went on without him. If he can't find the bus soon, he'll be stuck here in the present. It will make the grown-up me in the future really worry. I don't know what to do. Don't you have any advice?"

Grandma Leah sighed a big sigh. I think the part about the grown-up me worrying was what got her. Worrying is something Grandma Leah knows a lot about.

"All right," she said, "all right. Tell me, does he know what stops the bus is making?"

"No. He left the schedule on the bus."

"Well, has the bus stopped at the Empire State Building yet?"

I turned to Mack. He shook his head.

"All tour buses stop at the Empire State Building," she said. "It's a law they have. So go to the Empire State Building and you'll find your bus." She opened her purse and took out some money. "Here," she said. "Take a cab. My treat. I'd go with you myself, but my hair is wet. Also I can't stand crowds."

I looked at what she'd given me. A twenty-dollar bill!

"What if we go to the Empire State Building and we don't see the bus?" I asked.

"Then take the elevator to the top and look down. You can see everything from up there. Just promise me you won't stand too close to the railing. I don't want you falling and skinning your knee."

As we were leaving the beauty parlour, she called out to Mack, "Young man?"

"Yes?" said Mack.

"Don't you stand too close to the railing either."

"All right."

Grandma Leah may have had a rule about not talking to people from the future. But it didn't stop her from worrying about them.

Outside the beauty parlour, I tried to flag a cab. Then Mack did something I've never seen anybody do. He suddenly got dimmer, then brighter again. Like when you're watching TV and suddenly there's this kind of blip in the picture.

"Hey, how'd you do that?" I asked.

"How'd I do what?"

"You got dimmer, and then you got brighter again."

His eyes got very wide.

"You mean I *flickered*? Oh! Do you think this is what the teachers were talking about when they said something bad would happen? Maybe I *am* de-atomizing!" He flickered again. This time he laughed. "Hey, it kind of tickles," he said.

"Mack, this is nothing to laugh about," I said sternly. "You need to get serious about this." Whoa! I was beginning to sound like a real dad! "We've got to get to the Empire State Building and hope we find your bus!"

Chapter
Four

● ● ● ● ●

In the cab to the Empire State Building, Mack stopped flickering. What a relief! I sat back and took a closer look at him. Amazing. Mack even had a birthmark on his left cheek, like me.

"You know, Mack," I said, "suddenly having a son is very weird. But it's also kind of cool."

"Oh, that's peerless," said Mack.

"What is?"

"You just said something was 'cool'. I've never actually heard anybody use 'cool' in a sentence before. I mean I've read how kids used to say it all the time. But hearing you say it, it's, well . . . 'cool'." Mack laughed.

"Really?" I said. I wasn't sure I enjoyed being laughed at. "What are some words you guys use in the future?"

"Oh, 'peerless'," he said. "And 'splendid'."

Weird words, I thought. But in thirty years I'd probably think they were splendid. Then again, in thirty years I'd be old and a dad. So maybe I wouldn't.

"So, Mack, how am I as a dad? Splendid?"

"Oh, yeah, I guess. But sometimes you get mad at me for stuff like having a messy room and having to use the auto-sorter to clean it up. Or for eating too much insta-food. Or for leaving my clothes at other kids' houses and having to keep going to the teleporter to get them back. Stuff like that."

I didn't know which was weirder, hearing my future son say I was going to turn into somebody like my own dad, or hearing him talk about all these gadgets of the future.

Then it hit me! Mack knew all kinds of stuff! He knew who I was going to marry. Where I was going to live. And what I'd be as a grown-up. So he obviously must know if I'd be playing for the Yankees! Maybe I was on a World Series team!

"Uh, Mack, I can't help noticing your sweatshirt. Are you just a fan . . . or do I happen to play for the New York Yankees?"

Mack started to say something. Then he thought for a moment. And he stopped. He looked sorry. "I can't tell you that, Dad. We're not supposed to tell anybody from the past anything about their future. And that includes you."

"You can't tell me *anything* about my job?"

Mack shook his head.

"OK," I said. "But can I ask you just one thing?"

"What?"

"What kind of clothes do I wear at work?"

"Dad, come on. I'm not allowed to tell you stuff like that."

"OK. Tell me something else, then," I said. "Do you collect baseball cards?"

"Do *I* collect them? Sure. Screeners, though. Not cardboards."

"Screeners?" I said. "What's that?"

"The electronic ones. You never heard of screeners?"

"No."

"I can't believe it. I thought they already had screeners by the turn of the century. Each one has its own microcomputer in it. Cardboards like the Wade Boggs one are priceless antiques. That's why I was so upset when I lost the other one."

"Would you like to take some of my, uh, antique cardboards back with you?" I said.

Mack shook his head.

"Dad, nobody's allowed to make a profit

from time travel," he said sadly. "Too bad. But it's a rule."

"But if you promised me you'd never sell them," I said, "I don't see what could be wrong with it. I'll give you two packs of cardboards, if you just tell me whether I spend the off-season in Florida."

"Dad, stop it!" said Mack. "You really are being zardy! We're not even supposed to be discussing this kind of stuff."

"OK, OK," I said. "But what about who I marry?"

Mack hesitated. But then he said, "All I can tell you is that she's really splendid," he said. "And funny. And smart. And pretty. And . . ."

"And . . .?"

Suddenly the cab screeched to a stop.

We were at the Empire State Building.

My wife would have to wait. We had something more important to worry about – finding that double-decker tour bus.

We got out of the cab. Grandma Leah was right. The Empire State Building was surrounded by bright red double-decker buses. Every tour bus in the city must have been here.

"They all look alike!" I groaned.

"Don't worry, Dad," said Mack. "The bus isn't red. It's magenta and neon green – our school colours. You can't miss it."

Mack and I checked twice at both corners. But there was no magenta and neon green double-decker tour bus in sight. That was too bad, because Mack had started flickering again. He was starting to look like a human firefly!

"Let's go to the top floor and see if we can spot the bus," I said.

We were just heading for the doors when Mack noticed a hot-dog stand on the street corner.

"How peerless!" he said. "They're selling real hot dogs! Right out in the open!"

"You think it's weird they're selling hot dogs?"

"Well, they *are* illegal, Dad. Just like cigarettes and bacon. You could get them from a dog dealer, but they'd cost about six hundred dollars apiece. Plus mustard. And eating one is a misdemeanour, of course."

Mack smiled a sly smile.

"Dad, could you maybe buy me a—"

I couldn't hear the rest of what he was saying. He was flickering like crazy, and his

voice sounded full of static. Like when you're losing a radio station.

"Uh-oh," I said. "Mack, are you OK?"

"Yeah, I guess," he said once he was back to his normal self. But he didn't sound so sure. "Dad, I think maybe you're right. We'd better find that tour bus soon."

We hurried inside and took an elevator all the way up to the sight-seeing deck. It was jammed with tourists.

Mack leaned over the rail. Good thing Grandma Leah wasn't there to see that. We looked down at the streets below. We could see tiny ant-sized people and matchbox cars, but still no magenta and neon green bus. So far, we were getting nowhere fast.

"If I could only remember what our last stop was," Mack said. "I know it's

something to do with watches or clocks
. . . or time."

I pointed down to what looked like a green postage stamp.

"That's Central Park," I said. "The zoo is in there. They have a great clock."

Mack gave a flickering shake of his head.

"No, Central Park isn't the last stop," he said. Then all of a sudden he smiled. "But it is *one* of our stops," he said. "I'm sure of that!" Mack was excited now. "How long do you think it would take us to get there?"

"Well, Central Park is huge. Your bus could be lots of places. But there's a big entrance to the park at Columbus Circle."

"Let's try it," he said.

So we caught the first elevator down to

the ground floor and went back out onto the street.

"This is rush hour," I said. "A cab will take forever. Also, I've spent almost all of the money Grandma Leah gave me. But I still have enough for two subway tokens. Columbus Circle is just a few stops away."

"Oh, I'd love to ride the subway!" said Mack. "That's such an old-fashioned thing to do!"

So we headed for the nearest subway station. The platform was packed with people. A train pulled in right away. The doors slid open. But it didn't seem possible to fit even one more body into the subway car.

"Push!" I told Mack. I gave him a shove.

Mack squeezed his way into the car. The doors began closing.

"Hey! Wait for me!" I yelled.

I tried to force my way on. But the doors were too strong for me.

"Mack! Get off!" I yelled.

Mack tried to get off. But it was too late. The doors had closed. The train started pulling away, with me still on the platform.

"Get off at the next stop!" I screamed in through the window. "I'll take the next train and meet you there!"

Then the train was gone. Oh, great! What kind of father was I? I'd had a son for exactly one hour and fifteen minutes. And already I'd managed to lose him!

Chapter Five

●　●　●　●　●

The next train zoomed in with a roar. I shoved my way on and rode to the next stop. I got off and looked around. I couldn't see Mack. This was every parent's nightmare! What if he stood too close to the edge of the platform? What if the train came along . . .

I stopped myself. I was a worse worrier than Grandma Leah.

"Dad!" called a voice. I turned.

It was Mack! He was flickering in and out, but there he was!

"Thank heavens! You're safe!" I grabbed him and hugged him hard.

"Dad, will you cut it out? All these people are staring!"

"Sorry, son," I said. Son? I was actually calling him "son" now! And I was embarrassing him just the way my own dad embarrasses me. It's amazing how fast this fatherhood thing comes over you.

"Come on, Mack," I said. "We'd better get back on the next subway and head to Columbus Circle. It's just a few more stops from here."

"What stop are we at now?" Mack asked.

I shrugged and looked around. Where were we anyway? Then I saw the sign on the subway wall.

"We're at Times Square," I said.

Times Square.

Times Square!

Mack and I looked at each other. It was like bells and whistles were going off. This was the tour bus's last stop!

We raced up to the street, taking the stairs two at a time. We got to the street level. Mack was ahead of me.

"Dad! I think I see it!" he said. He was flickering like crazy now. And his voice was really fading in and out.

Yes! There it was! Coming around the corner of 42nd Street and Broadway. A two-tone magenta and neon green double-decker bus! We'd found it in time!

Mack turned to me. "Well, Dad," he said, "I guess this is goodbye."

I nodded. "Weird," I said. "I won't get to see you again for like another twenty years."

"Dad, I'll be back home in less than an hour," said Mack. "We'll see each other then."

"Not exactly," I said. "The grown-up me will see you then. But not this me. This me won't see you again until you're born."

I sighed.

You might think I'm crazy for feeling sad. Probably you won't understand till you're a parent yourself. So in the meantime, you'll just have to trust me on this.

"Here, Dad," said Mack. "I want you to have this."

He dug in his pocket and handed me the rookie card. My eyes grew wide. There was Wade Boggs staring up at me, smiling. What a card! But I couldn't take it.

"You keep it, Mack," I said. "When you get back home, I don't want you to get in trouble with me."

"Dad, you are splendid!" he said. Then he ran towards the bus.

A couple of his friends spotted Mack. He motioned for them to distract the teacher's attention. When the teacher wasn't looking, Mack sneaked onto the bus.

A second later he was waving goodbye to me from a window. I waved back. He didn't seem to be flickering any more, thank goodness.

"Have a good trip!" I called.

"Thanks, Dad!"

"Make sure you have your seatbelt on!" I called. I didn't know what else to say to him.

I watched the bus slowly start to fade. At first it looked just a little blurred. Then you could see right through it.

"Bye, Dad!" I heard Mack shout.

I decided to give it one last try.

"Since I'm such a splendid father," I yelled, "can't you at least tell me my future wife's name?"

The bus had almost totally disappeared. But I heard Mack's last words.

"Sure, Dad," he called. "It's . . . Mom."

Chapter Six

● ● ● ● ●

The next day we had our family reunion. My dad made me wear a suit. It was great seeing all my uncles and aunts and cousins from Chicago and a bunch of other cities. Grandma Leah looked very nice with her new hairdo.

"Just look at this boy!" said my Aunt Sadie from San Diego. "He looks so grown up in that suit. I almost

mistook him for Uncle Milton!"

She squeezed my cheek. Is squeezing cheeks supposed to be fun for the squeezer or the squeezee?

"In just a few years," said Aunt Sadie, "Zack will be getting married and having a son of his own. Would you like that, Zack? To have a son of your own?"

"I have one already," I said. "And he's a great kid."

Aunt Sadie laughed and gave me another cheek squeeze. The bruises lasted around a week.

But that same week I got a call from Fred at the card store.

"Good news, Zack," he said. "Another Wade Boggs rookie card just came in. You want it?"

"You bet," I said. "Even though in

thirty-two years my son will take it to school and lose it. But then he'll come back here from the future and buy me another one."

There was a short pause on the other end of the line.

"Yeah, OK, I got a call on my other phone, kid," he said, and hung up.

I happen to know Fred only has one phone.

What else happens to Zack?

Find out in

NEVER TRUST A CAT
WHO WEARS EARRINGS

Suddenly I thought about all the weird stuff I'd been doing – licking up spilled milk, sleeping all curled up on the floor, sneaking up on birds. It all started to make sense.

"Dad," I said in a scared voice. "You know what I think is happening to me?"

"What?" said Dad.

"I think I'm turning into a cat!" I said.

THE ZACK FILES

Read all of Zack's weird adventures!

All Macmillan titles can be ordered at your local bookshop
or are available by post from:

**Book Service by Post
PO Box 29, Douglas, Isle of Man IM99 1BO**

Credit cards accepted. For details:
Telephone: 01624 675137
Fax: 01624 670923
E-mail: bookshop@enterprise.net

Free postage and packing in the UK.
Overseas customers: add £1 per book (paperback)
and £3 per book (hardback).

The prices shown are correct at the time of going to press. However,
Macmillan Publishers reserve the right to show new retail prices on
covers which may differ from those previously advertised.